Foreword by N̶.̶

She's Just Like Me

The Dating Chronicles of Women

written by

Ayanna Jackson, M.Ed

First paperback edition
ISBN (for paperback): 978-1-7333032-0-0
ISBN (for audible): 978-1-7333032-1-7

Book Design by kozakura (www.fiverr.com/kozakura)
Book Editor by Lucretia Manners

Contents

Foreword   i

Acknowledgements   v

A Special Note to You   1

Chronicle One

Damaged Goods   5

Reflective Questions   10

Chronicle Two

The Danger Zone   13

Reflective Questions   20

Chronicle Three

Finding B.E.A.U.T.Y.   23

Reflective Questions   29

Chronicle Four

Lost But Found   31

Reflective Questions   39

Chronicle Five

The One   43

Reflective Questions   53

The Breakthrough   57

Foreword

When the author asked me to write the Foreword for, *She's Just Like Me: The Dating Chronicles of Women*, I was elated, proud and honored.

Elated because I can tell you first-hand that this book is equipped and filled with tools and strategies that will help any woman--- whether dating, single, or married-- to sustain in a world where relationships are perceptually different but really are the same.

I was proud and honored because as her mom, I can finally say she listened. After watching her grow and evolve through childhood into her adult years, I experienced her dating life, setbacks, heartaches, break ups, and remembered her doubts about ever getting married. Ayanna, with her uncanny vulnerability to talk about her life experiences while dating certainly takes you on a journey not only of her life, but a journey every woman has and will travel.

This book is so relatable that I found myself thinking back and wishing if I'd had this book during the time I went through the difficulties of abuse, losses, and eventually divorce with her father, perhaps things could have been a little different for me. I could have recognized the signs that were there before I said "I do" to her father at 18. Perhaps, I would not have made the mistakes that I made of staying too long, accepting the abuse, limiting my standards, and not believing in my self-worth. This book, is definitely a MUST read.

As I stated earlier, the author takes you on a journey not only about her life, but also the life of a woman who recognizes her faults, flaws, strengths and weaknesses, and identifies the balance and healing needed to move on in life. Reading this book, will allow you to identify with different stages within your relationship, recognize hidden signs and red flags, and understand a flawed and damaged relationship when you are in it. You will be able to escape that woman that allows herself to fall into the trap of damaged goods and danger zones.

You will be able to discover your losses and identify the traps that keep you feeling lonely, vulnerable and ashamed. As you journey through this book, you will not only be able to see yourself, but you will also be able to reflect and truly journal your way through these stories to rescue the girl inside of you and find the woman you truly desire to be.

I wholeheartedly believe that when you begin to read, *She's Just Like Me: The Dating Chronicles of Women,* you will see how the author utilizes her real-life experiences to unfold in so many ways that will help every woman reading this book identify with themselves. You will begin to see that this book was indeed under construction years before now.

She's Just Like Me is evidence that women of all ages, colors, and creeds can gain knowledge, wisdom, and apply new meaning to the reflection questions presented within the book. If answered

Foreword

When the author asked me to write the Foreword for, *She's Just Like Me: The Dating Chronicles of Women,* I was elated, proud and honored.

Elatéd because I can tell you first-hand that this book is equipped and filled with tools and strategies that will help any woman--- whether dating, single, or married-- to sustain in a world where relationships are perceptually different but really are the same.

I was proud and honored because as her mom, I can finally say she listened. After watching her grow and evolve through childhood into her adult years, I experienced her dating life, setbacks, heartaches, break ups, and remembered her doubts about ever getting married. Ayanna, with her uncanny vulnerability to talk about her life experiences while dating certainly takes you on a journey not only of her life, but a journey every woman has and will travel.

This book is so relatable that I found myself thinking back and wishing if I'd had this book during the time I went through the difficulties of abuse, losses, and eventually divorce with her father, perhaps things could have been a little different for me. I could have recognized the signs that were there before I said "I do" to her father at 18. Perhaps, I would not have made the mistakes that I made of staying too long, accepting the abuse, limiting my standards, and not believing in my self-worth. This book, is definitely a MUST read.

As I stated earlier, the author takes you on a journey not only about her life, but also the life of a woman who recognizes her faults, flaws, strengths and weaknesses, and identifies the balance and healing needed to move on in life. Reading this book, will allow you to identify with different stages within your relationship, recognize hidden signs and red flags, and understand a flawed and damaged relationship when you are in it. You will be able to escape that woman that allows herself to fall into the trap of damaged goods and danger zones.

You will be able to discover your losses and identify the traps that keep you feeling lonely, vulnerable and ashamed. As you journey through this book, you will not only be able to see yourself, but you will also be able to reflect and truly journal your way through these stories to rescue the girl inside of you and find the woman you truly desire to be.

I wholeheartedly believe that when you begin to read, *She's Just Like Me: The Dating Chronicles of Women,* you will see how the author utilizes her real-life experiences to unfold in so many ways that will help every woman reading this book identify with themselves. You will begin to see that this book was indeed under construction years before now.

She's Just Like Me is evidence that women of all ages, colors, and creeds can gain knowledge, wisdom, and apply new meaning to the reflection questions presented within the book. If answered

She's Just Like Me

The Dating Chronicles of Women

She's Just Like Me

The Dating Chronicles of Women

honestly, these reflection questions can serve as a tool and strategy to help any woman overcome the traps, damaged goods, danger zones, and avoidable signs necessary to heal, and recognize Mr. Right. It is my desire that after reading this book, your story will end as the author's, who was able to recognize her soul-mate because she became whole from the inside out.

She's Just Like Me: The Dating Chronicles of Women, was written by a woman who truly demonstrates a woman spending time journaling daily and writing the vision given to her from God.

Whether you are dating, single, married or coming out of a divorce, you will be able to see yourself through the eyes of at least one of the women, if not all of the women throughout this book. The refreshing authenticity displayed in this book by the author will help you recognize your not so refining moments, reject the lie that you will never find true love, discover practical ways to connect with your inner-self, and embrace yourself as the masterpiece and work in progress.

The Author is the founder of Finding B.E.A.U.T.Y., Co-founder of 97Credit alongside her husband, real estate agent, and educator. She is a wife, daughter, and sister.

Monique Smith, MBA

CEO/Founder P Visions Incorporated DBA Panoramic Visions
Mother of Author

A Special Note to You

To my beautiful, smart, intelligent queens, you are worth it! No matter your age, no matter your walk of life, this book was written to inspire and encourage you to not give up on your end relationship goals. If you have ever wondered, "Am I good enough?" This book was written for you. If you have ever questioned yourself asking, "When is my time for love going to come?" This book was written for you. If you have ever questioned your self-worth, this book was written for you.

To every woman who has struggled in her singleness, has been afraid of loneliness, has longed for someone to fill that void, or has held yourself so tight as you rock yourself to sleep, this book is for you.

She's Just Like Me will allow you to read different relationship stories that real women have experienced. Within this book of short stories, you will be able to self-reflect, self-evaluate, and create solutions to some of your challenges.

My hope is to help at least one woman journey through her emotions, insecurities, and ways of thinking to identify patterns of behavior that tend to keep you bounded to negative, toxic relationships. These stories should help you understand that, *She's Just Like Me*, and that we have all experienced the good, the bad, and the ugly within relationships.

I am a firm believer that when you first discover Finding Boldness Excellence and Uniqueness Through You, you will be one step closer to finding the woman that you were destined to be.

Ayanna Jackson,

Founder of: Finding B.E.A.U.T.Y

Finding Boldness Excellence and Uniqueness Through You

CHRONICLE
ONE

Damaged Goods

Here I was once again in another wedding alone, tipsy, and hopeless. This time, it was my best friend getting married, so I had to keep it together for her. In the midst of keeping it together, I so desperately wondered if it would ever be my time to find the man of my dreams to spend the rest of my life with.

For a moment I daydreamed how my wedding day would be. No bridesmaids, no flower girls, no groomsmen, just my groom waiting on me at the altar. I pictured myself walking down in a rose lace and diamond studded dress, with a six-foot train and a rose lace and diamond studded veil attached to the back of my hair.

I saw everyone that was in the room. My mother, my father getting ready to walk me down the aisle, all of my friends, and family smiling at me as I stood at the top of the stairs. Slowly, walking down the aisle to India Arie, "*Beautiful Surprise*," I finally reach my groom. I stare into his eyes and before the pastor can even utter the words, "I now pronounce you husband and wife," I kiss him so passionately as if it were just us in the room. As we kiss, the claps get louder and louder as if they want us to continue giving them a show. I hear someone say, "This is just so beautiful. They look so good together, don't you think, Grace?"

That's when it hit me, I'm 34 and still not married; with no kids to call my own. Here I am at my third wedding in less than six months apart, and not one has been mine. I smile and nod and say yes, they are, I am so happy for them. After the ceremony proceeded, and all the roles and duties of the bridesmaids were finished, I made my way outside to get some fresh air.

In that moment, I began to ask God what was wrong with me. "Why haven't You allowed me to find a man to fulfill my needs?" I am so sick of being lonely and for once I just wanted someone—anyone-- to want me. I desperately longed for that void to be filled with a man that could just take me away from all of my frustrations.

Just before the tears came rolling down, I heard this deep voice say, "Is everything ok with you?" As I looked up, I saw a 6'2, dark skinned, slim but built, sexy man in my view. I sniffed up my tears and said, "Yes, just allergies. You know how the weather can be. I'm sorry you are?" "I'm Jason, a friend of the groom. We went to college together, and I'm just here to support him on his new journey. I saw you in the wedding looking really beautiful; how come you are not inside with everyone else?"

Lying and nervous, I replied, "I just needed some fresh air and I got a phone call and it was really loud inside. Why are you outside? Shouldn't you be partying it up with ya boy, celebrating?" Laughing, he replied, "I actually had to run out to my car to get my phone." I said, "Oh, ok. Well, I'll see you later." He extended his hand and said, "No, you are getting ready to come with me.

The weather looks like it's getting ready to get bad. Besides, I may wanna see some of your moves on the dance floor."

I thought to myself how I hadn't heard anyone say anything like that to me in a while. I had been longing for some fine man to come along and give me some attention, and here it was happening for me right here and now. I got up, pulled my gold tight fitting sequin dress down, and proceeded to enter back into the reception. Jason and I danced all night long.

For once, I was happy and felt at peace. I thought to myself as he pulled me closer to him, and began breathing softly into my neck, could this be the answer to my prayers? After we danced the night away and the bride and groom drove off into their new journey together, Jason put his hands around my waist and whispered, "So what are your plans once you leave here?" Excited, yet nervous, I looked at him with a straight face and said, "Well it depends. Where are you taking me?"

If one thing I knew, it was how to flirt. I never had a problem getting a man; I just couldn't figure out where to meet them. Now that I had Jason in front of me, I knew I was going to take advantage of the opportunity. He smiled and said, "Follow me, I'm going to take you somewhere extra special."

We hopped in our cars and I proceeded to follow him. I had to admit I was quite impressed with his car. He drove a 2017 Lexus ES all black with dark tinted windows. I hadn't been inside of his car, but from the looks of him I could tell that he took pride in making sure his car was always well kept.

Finally, after driving about 30 minutes out, we made it to our destination. It was a small hole in the wall, and I could hear the sounds of of one of my favorite old school jams from the 80s' playing as he opened up my car door. He said, "I wanna see more of those moves you had earlier today, so I figured I'd bring you here to my spot. I had never heard of this place before. I smiled and nodded and told him, "You haven't seen nothing yet."

Once we made it inside, we danced all night long, to the point where the lights began to come on. As we looked around and we were one of the last ones left in the place, we just fell into each other's arms and laughed. Jason looked at me and pulled me close to him and said, "Grace, I really don't want this night to end. We are having too much fun and I'm really enjoying you." Knowing that I should not have said what I said because I knew where it was going to lead, I looked him in his eyes and told him, "It doesn't have to."

We got in our cars and I followed him to his apartment. He lived in a gated building so right there, I felt safe and secure knowing that I was with him. He let me park my car in his garage and we went upstairs. We wasted no time either. From the stairs, to the couch, to the kitchen counter, to the dining room table, to the bed, to the floor, from the floor to the shower; Jason gave me what I wanted. I knew that what I was doing was wrong, but in the moment of being wrong, it just felt so right, he felt right, WE felt right.

The next morning after our rendezvous was over, he made us a nice breakfast, and we just talked and laughed and enjoyed each other's company. After a couple of hours went by, he told me that he had to be leaving in the next hour so he needed to get dressed and cleaned up so that he could be gone. I grabbed my belongings and thanked him for a wonderful night, and he leaned in and kissed me on top of my forehead.

As I walked down the stairs, he grabbed my arm, pulled me close and said, "I really enjoyed you. I'll call you." Once I left his place, I never heard from him again. I called the next day, and he didn't respond. I called back to back the following day, and still no response. I even went so far as to send a "thinking of you text" but he still didn't respond.

After a moment, I just sat there on the edge of my bed thinking how I could have allowed myself to fall in this trap all over again. There I was alone, lonely, sad, and still damaged.

Reflect on the following dating story.

1. Have you ever been in this situation before? How many times?

_____
_____
_____
_____
_____
_____
_____
_____
_____
_____
_____

2. If you have ever faced rejection, how were you made to feel?

_____
_____
_____
_____
_____
_____
_____
_____
_____
_____

3. What steps did you take to overcome and heal from your rejection?

_____

_____

_____

_____

_____

_____

_____

_____

4. What specific requests do you have regarding your existing or pre-existing relationship?

_____

_____

_____

_____

_____

_____

_____

_____

_____

_____

_____

_____

Chronicle
Two

The Danger Zone

This is my time, I thought to myself. I had just taken a new job and already within six months I was receiving a new promotion. "Stacey, we would like to take the time out and thank you for all of your hard work and efforts. We are honored to name you as our new Director of Finance."

As everyone in the conference room applauded, I stood up and looked around the room. For a moment, I just embraced the idea that I was one of three Black women in that position, and it felt good. "Thank you all for this opportunity, I am so honored to hold this position and I am extremely confident that our company is going to continue to grow more than what we could ever have imagined."

Once I made it back to my desk, I gathered up all of my belongings and headed to the dealership. I was now trading my *Audi* in for something a little more Director-ish. Out I came with the new 2019 *Maserati*, white on chrome and the interior was ice white with black leather trim. Oh, it was just something about that new car smell that really got me going. I was so super thankful and super proud of myself that I just began to thank God for His wonderful blessings. I knew that none of this could be possible without His grace and mercy.

As I drove off the lot, I realized how good it felt to be solely focused on me. I began putting my life into a new perspective. I started back working out, I wasn't eating out as much, and I had enjoyed my eight-month hiatus from men and dating. I had been putting my self-worth first, and it sure was feeling good. My efforts to focus solely on me were paying off and I was enjoying the reaping of the benefits. I had decided to take a step back from guys and dating because I really wanted to explore my needs and wants. Plus, I was so sick and tired of the same games.

After about two months into my new job, I decided to put myself back on the dating scene, but this time, I was going in with a new attitude. I actually had gotten this dating game down to a science and for once I could say I was learning the game. I would meet guys that were cool, have great conversation, and we would just kick it and have a good time.

For once, I did not have to worry about giving something up to feel wanted. I was beginning to realize that I had a certain type of inner power that could be used at my disposal and on my terms. It wasn't until about three months in the new position that I met my test. Upon initially meeting him, I thought, "Ugh, this guy is not type. He looks like he is only 5'8 and he's a little round and stocky."

I remember talking to my friend, Shay, and she explained to me that this was part of my problem. She said, "This is why you are still single." I said, "No it's not I choose to be single. I'm not going to force myself to be into someone that is totally not my type. " "Not your type," Shay replied. It doesn't matter girl, the whole purpose of dating is to get out there and try different flavors of the water, not just stick to one particular kind from the tap." "Hahahaha!" I exclaimed. "This doesn't even make any sense. However, if you say I need to give it a try, I will. After all, I'm not trying to close myself into a box."

The next morning at work, I saw the guy again. He stopped me as I was walking down the hall. "Hey how you doing this morning?" he asked. Not interested and a little annoyed, I answered, "I'm good..." Interjecting he said, "Carter, my name is Carter." Smiling, I said, "Well nice to meet you, I'm Stacey. What floor do you work on, Carter? I've never seen you here on the 12th floor before." Stuttering he said, "Oh, no, I'm down on the 3rd floor in Maintenance." I thought to myself, "Maintenance, now what do I look like being involved with a guy from maintenance?"

I just smiled and nodded, "Oh, ok, well I really have to get going. I have a meeting that starts in the next 20 minutes. Carter, it was very nice to finally put a name to the face."

After the meeting, I grabbed my phone and called Shay to tell her what had just happened and without even allowing me to get the story fully out of mouth, she cuts me off and starts up. Shay yelled, "See this is your problem, you are always looking at guys like they are your 'forever guy'. No, just go out a few times with him and get what you can get out of him and keep it moving, just have fun." As I sat there allowing Shay to yell at me, I thought to myself, "Shay's right. Especially since I'll just keep him around as a friend?"

A few months passed, and Carter and I became an unofficial couple. I couldn't believe how much fun we actually had together. I really grew to like him and felt myself slowly falling hard for him. I didn't know what it was about him, but he was different from the rest. I guess Shay was right; I just needed to go outside of my comfort zone.

As time went on, I began noticing little things about him. I quickly noticed that he always needed to be around me. At first, I thought this was a good thing because we spent a lot of time together, but as time went on, he became possessive.

Yelling as I walked towards the door he said. "Where you going?" In shock and a little nervous, I yelled back, "I'm just going to the store. I need to get some things to cook for tonight." Frustrated and demanding, he asked, "Well who you going with? The last time you went to the store, it took you too long and you were gone for about two hours." Ignoring him, I just walked off. As I headed towards the door, he yelled, "You need to answer your phone too, because I'm about to call you!" In my mind, I knew this wasn't normal, but I did enjoy the time we spent together so I figured it wasn't too bad.

The arguing and the foolishness worsened as time went on. One Sunday after church, I decided to go and meet my mother at her house. I figured I'd drop off her cake pan that she had let me borrow two weeks earlier. Of course, Carter was with me, as he always was. We argued the whole way there. "Why were you giving that dude a hug after the service? How long have you been knowing him?" "What are you talking about?" I yelled back. "Why are you making something out of nothing? I have known him for about three years, and we used to serve on the youth board together." "Well the next time you need to make sure you introduce me."

Pissed off, I parked the car, got the cake pan out the back and proceeded to the door. He opened his door and followed behind. I'll be honest, I had no intent on him meeting my mother that day, but because I did not want to make things worse with him, I just let it ride. It's like my mom could smell trouble because she opened her door on the first ring.

"Hey, Mama, how are you?" "I'm good, how are you and who is this?" She looked Carter up and down with a look that I had never seen before. "Mama, this is Carter, this is my fr..." "Boyfriend," he interjected. "Boyfriend? And just when did you get a boyfriend?" Shocked and caught off guard, I said, "We have been dating for about three months. We are still getting to know each other." After I said that, I could tell that comment pissed him off because he cut his eyes at me like he wanted to curse me out.

As we were getting ready to leave, she pulled me back and said, "Stacey, I do not have a good feeling about him at all. Something about him seems controlling, jealous, and possessive. I really think you need to reconsider this with him; I just don't see anything good coming out of this."

I knew my mom was right, but I ignored her and said, "Mama I know what I'm doing, I'm going to be fine." If only I had put my pride to the side and listened to my mom. If only I had taken heed to her warning. If only I had not tried to prove her wrong, maybe I could have spared three years of my life. Just maybe I would have known not to enter into the danger zone.

More and more, I began to recognize things that were making me feel like Carter was hiding some things from me. I noticed that he wasn't getting up and going to work anymore. After two weeks, I finally learned that he was fired because of his aggressive behavior. I told him that he needed to get some help, but he yelled at me and told me that he didn't have a problem.

A year went by and there were still signs of Carter hiding things from me, but I thought he would change for me, so I stayed. I stayed so long that I didn't even recognize myself when I looked in the mirror. I was beginning to lose myself in him, trying to help save him from himself, and in return I began to slowly deteriorate. I found myself becoming so lazy and losing my drive and ambition. I began to miss work because he wanted me to stay home with him. All he wanted was for us to lay up and be under each other all day. I had missed so much work within the past few months that I was missing important deadlines and assignments.

My boss called me into the office. "Stacey, we need to talk. It seems like there have been some serious changes in your behavior. You don't seem motivated or enthused, it's almost like you have lost yourself. Is it the stress of the job?" Worried, I exclaimed, "I assure you, Mr. Trevino that I am not stressed. I just had a real rough couple of months, but I'm better now.

I could not believe that I had actually allowed myself to get so caught up into a guy to where I began to lose sight of my purpose. Through all of that I still did not have the strength to leave Carter. I felt like if I left him, then I would be incomplete. Here I was with a new job, nice home, and so much going for myself, I just didn't want to not have a man there to enjoy it with. Sadly enough, I stayed.

Another year went by and I was still with Carter, unhappy and all. I felt that if I stayed, then I would be able to prove my mother, my friends, and even myself wrong. All I had to do was make him see that my heart was pure and that I wanted the best for him and then he would change for me...right?

Reflect on the following dating story.

1. Make a list of the red flags/warning signs that you may have noticed and ignored in your relationship.

_____

_____

_____

_____

_____

_____

_____

_____

2. Why do/did you stay in a situation (s) that you are /were not comfortable with?

_____

_____

_____

_____

_____

_____

_____

_____

3. Are you afraid of lonely? Why or why not?

_____

_____

_____

_____

_____

_____

_____

_____

_____

_____

4. What made you stay? What would you have changed about the situation?

_____

_____

_____

_____

_____

_____

_____

_____

_____

_____

_____

_____

Chronicle
Three

Finding B.E.A.U.T.Y.

Once I graduated, from college, I moved back home to save money and find a full-time job. My mother was very supportive throughout this journey because she allowed me to get myself together. She only had one condition and that was for me to save my paychecks so that when I got on my feet, I'd be set. I was very thankful, to say the least. I didn't know too many parents who would allow their child to come back home, save their entire check, and not pay any bills. This was the life!

About six months after graduation, I received a long-term substitute teaching position at a local elementary school. I felt this would be the time of my life and just the fresh start I needed to rejuvenate me.

Although I had found a job doing what I loved to do, meeting new friends and catching up with old ones, I still found myself sad and incomplete. In my mind, I was still lacking a boyfriend, friend, companion, or just someone to look at. I began to feel myself slowly drifting back into that state of depression that I had once felt so long ago. I was still trying to fill a void with a man instead of filling that void with myself.

During my spring break I was due to have surgery and what was also approaching, my 25th birthday. I soon learned there were three things you just should not mix together: surgery, a year older, and no man! It sounds funny, but I was so depressed because here I was 25, still single, no relationship, not even a conversation. To make matters worse, I couldn't get out the house and do anything because of the surgery that had just taken place. Talk about lots of time on my hands.

I started feeling like the legendary Lenny Williams, *"I watched television until television went off,"* talk about lonely!!!! My mom allowed me to mope around for a couple of days until finally she couldn't stand to see me like that anymore. She came in my room, flipped the light switch on, and yelled, "Reese, get up!" I knew she was mad because she called me Reese. She never called me Reese when she was happy and things were good; I was always her Sha'Reese. "Why?" I exclaimed. "It is 5:oo in the morning and I just want to be left alone!" I suddenly felt the cold air whip across my skin as she snatched the covers off of me and demanded that I get up now. She stated, "If I have to drag you out this bed every morning, I will! I will not allow you to walk around and feel sorry for yourself any longer."

Huffing and puffing, I got out of bed and followed her to her room. When I entered into her room, it was pitch black and soft music playing as if you were laying on a massage table getting a massage.

Although the room was dark, there was a sense of peace and serenity. She walked me to her bed and sat me on the edge.

She whispered, "Sit and close your eyes. Let go of all the hurt and pain that you have. Release it. Let it go."

Sitting there I began to think about all of my struggles, my heartaches, my bad decisions, my insecurities, my flaws, and everything else that one could think. I then began to cry and I heard her say, "That's it, let it go." When I heard those words, again I began to cry even harder because I knew it was time to let go of all those struggles from the past and move forward. My mother then prayed for me and I just wrapped my arms around her as if I were a little girl with ponytails and ribbons. I heard the words from God say to me, "Everything will be fine. Now you just have to trust and believe." Once I heard those comforting words, I began to straighten myself up.

Once I had calmed down, she turned the television on, and a known pastor was doing one of his motivational words. We didn't catch the entire service, but what I did hear were words that pierced my soul and continued to stick with me, leaving my eyes wide open. The pastor said, "For those of you that feel time is passing you up and you still haven't found Mr. Right or Mrs. Right, I'm here to tell you that it is on its way, but you have to be patient and wait on God to lead you. While you are in your holding place, go and place an empty picture frame next to your bed."

When he said this I thought, "What is so significant about an empty frame?" He went on to say, "I bet you some of you are thinking, why an empty frame? Well, that empty frame will be your placeholder for your Mr. or Mrs. Right. When that time comes---because it will come--- that frame that you waited so patiently to be filled will be filled with memories of the one who you will spend the rest of your life with." I thought, "WOW!!!"

Something so small had so much value. I thanked my mom for her ability to get me away from myself and limped on back to my room to find an empty frame to place by my bed.

After my mind-blowing experience, I began to really truthfully explore myself and find my B.E.A.U.T.Y. I knew that in order for this journey to be worthwhile, I had to be honest with my emotions and myself. I began reflecting back on my years of dating and began to discover that many of my issues started when I was 12.

I remembered watching my mom stay in such a toxic relationship for years. I, in turn, thought that represented how you showed love to someone by sticking it out with him even though it wasn't healthy. I then realized that I had been making decisions that shaped my dating life for years to come based on what my inner 12-year-old girl had experienced. I did not realize that all the toxicity I saw from when I was 12 had impacted me all these years.

From here, I started by making a list of Do's and Don'ts for new relationships based on all of my relationships from the past. This opened my eyes wide because I was now starting to see a pattern within myself. I had more Don'ts than I did Do's. Although this was shocking and a little embarrassing to see and admit, I knew this was the start I needed in order to experience the new journey to find me.

The next thing I did was made a list of realistic goals. It consisted of short term and long-term goals and ranged from the age that I would be married; all the way to how many books I would read.

From there, I began reading a Christian based book by Joshua Harris, *I Kissed Dating Goodbye*. This book focused on the importance of dating, exploring, and understanding the true you. The book forced me to become consumed with myself that even the idea of dating an outside force would be seemingly impossible. Once I became comfortable with myself and began to focus my energy and attention on me, I began to read another novel that related to the "worldly" aspects of dating, *Hand- me-down heartache* by Tajuana Butler.

These two books helped me explore myself through the eyes of being single, the mistakes often made while dating, learning how to enjoy the upsides of being single, and discovering the real meaning of true love not just for myself, but with my soulmate.

For the first time in a long time, I found myself engaging, desiring, and wanting no one but me. I began spending intentional time exploring what made me laugh, cry, smile, shut down, and talk louder. I began taking myself on dates, like literally on a movie and dinner date by myself. Yes, this was very intimidating because I had never done this before, but I knew this was the start of my new beginning.

The funny thing I found about going out to eat by myself was that it made the waitress or waiter feel bad for me because I was alone. It never failed they either gave me a free drink or dessert. I slowly began to not feel so lonely anymore because I was enjoying me.

Every Saturday, I would find myself at a restaurant with my note pad and laptop and just engaging in me. The more I did it, the more comfortable I became in my own skin, and that was one of the ways I knew I was getting one step closer to successfully completing my journey of finding my true B.E.A.U.T.Y. --- Boldness Excellence and Uniqueness Through You.

Reflect on the following dating chronicle.

1. How has your inner girl shaped the woman who you are today?

_____

_____

_____

_____

_____

_____

_____

_____

_____

2. Make a list of goals that are very explicit and detail what you truly want have and what you truly want to do.

_____

_____

_____

_____

_____

_____

_____

_____

_____

_____

_____

_____

Chronicle
Four

Lost But Found

"Ding, Ding, Ding." As the alarm sounded, I hit the snooze button so I didn't have to face reality. Today, July 6th, marked the day that I would always remember. In just two hours I would be standing before a judge and next to my attorney to dissolve my marriage. This was the day that I realized I would be walking away from 20 years of marriage, a beautiful family of four, a huge custom-built house, and the life that everyone in my circle aspired to have.

As I got dressed, so many questions began to run through my mind. What will I say if I see him on today? How am I going to break the news to the kids that Mommy and Daddy are really divorced for good? What will my friends and family think of me? What will my kids think of me? Will my kids think it was my fault that their dad and I weren't together anymore? What will the people in the church think when they hear that my husband of 20 years is no longer that?

It was a sad death, but on the flip side of that coin, it would be a day of freedom from the abuse, the silent treatment, the feeling of always walking on edge, and the overall stress that Bryce brought into our marriage.

As I pulled into the parking lot of the courthouse, my heart began to beat so fast that I felt that I was going to hyperventilate. I did not know what to expect because I had never gone through anything like this. Bryce was the only man that I had been with since high school and I just felt so lost in this moment. I had no idea as to how I was going to piece together my life as a single woman with two children.

Walking through the security monitors, I saw my attorney waiting on me. "How are you this morning?" She hugged me so tightly that I just took a deep breath and held on to her. "I'm ok," I explained, "Just trying to be strong and make it through this day." "Oh Christine, you are going to be fine. I promise that I'm going to see you through this. You are going to be ok. Is there someone here to accompany you?"

Looking up at her, it hit me. I had no one there by my side to support me as I traveled down this road of distraught, loneliness, hurt, and pain. I had no familiar face with me as I sat inside the courtroom waiting for my case to be called on the docket.

"All rise!" the bailiff exclaimed. In walked the judge in his long black gown. He was a taller, slim fit judge; not the usual judge that one would often see. I always imagined judges being older and not so tall; at least that's what the television always showed. "On the 9:00 am docket, we have Christine Stone vs. Bryce Stone. Will both parties please approach the bench?" Looking around the courtroom, I did not see Bryce and I wondered if he was even going to show. With my attorney holding out her hand, I grabbed it and we approached the bench.

"Christine," Judge Snyder said. "Today you are here for the dissolution of your marriage is that correct?" Holding back the tears, I answered, "Yes, yes sir it is". "Well Mrs. Stone, it appears that your husband did not show for the hearing to contest anything, so I will be asking you three questions and after your responses, I will grant the divorce final. Do you have any questions before we begin?" Looking at my attorney in tears, I replied, "No sir."

The judge pulled out a sheet of paper and began reading off the questions, "Question one, have you consummated over the last 30 days with your husband?" I thought back to the wonderful love we used to make. This area was never a problem for us. Bryce did it for me, I did it for him and we honestly did it for each other. Our love-making was so passionate, and honestly, that was what I was going to miss most about him. Wherever he wanted it, I would give it to him. On the couch, in the car, on the table, in the tub, you name it; I was on it. Looking at the judge, I answered with a direct, "No."

"Ok, question two, have you both resided in the household within the last 30 days?" Tears began to run down my face as I thought about the last time Bryce and I were in the same house together. That was the day that I thought I was going to lose my life. He had come home that night drunk and upset because I hadn't answered his calls because my battery had run dead. He came in the house, yelled my name, as soon as I turned the corner, all I felt was an open hand going across my face.

Caught off guard and trying to catch my breath, I screamed, "What the hell is wrong with you?" You told me you would never put your hands on me again! What is your problem?" With no words from him, he just continued to pound my face with his fist and all I could taste was the blood that was running down from nose to my mouth.

Escaping his fist, I tried to run upstairs to my daughter's room, but he caught my leg and pulled me back down. Hearing the screams of horror, my daughter ran past us on the stairs to the kitchen, grabbed a butcher knife and yelled, "Get off of my Mama! Daddy, if you do not stop and leave, I will take this knife and kill you!"

Backing up, he looked at her with the strangest look and ran down the stairs into our bedroom. Without thinking twice, I grabbed my children's bag of clothes and ran out of that house never looking back. Looking at the judge with a well full of tears, I said, "No!"

"Ok Mrs. Stone, this is my third and final question for you. Do you see you two getting back together?" Out of all of the questions, I answered this one so fast and swift, my attorney and the judge looked at me with slight surprise, "No." "Well Mrs. Stone, I now grant your request and you are, in eyes of the court of law, officially divorced." The banging of the gavel revealed that my marriage of 20 years was officially over.

That chapter of my life ended at 9:05 that morning. I looked at the judge stunned, thinking, "That's it?" My entire marriage of 20 years that felt as if it took an entire lifetime to build took only five minutes to end. Relieved, yet scared, I looked into my attorney's eyes with fear as if I were a little girl. She hugged me so tightly and I thanked her for her presence and time.

After we hugged and made our way towards the courtroom exit, Judge Snyder said, "Miss Christine, please do take care of yourself. I promise you; this pain is going to pass." In tears, I nodded my head and said thank you.

As I made it to the café down the street, I sat in the car to gather myself and thought, "What do I do now?" What do you do when death suddenly comes knocking at your door? Making my way inside of the restaurant, I felt as though everyone was staring at me. It's almost like they all knew what had just happened to me an hour ago. Was it in my head, was I tripping? I mean, surely, they can't know. "How many in your party?" the hostess asked. Quietly and nervously I answered, "Just one." As she showed me to my seat, I immediately put my head down in my menu as if I was really trying to read for items that I wanted to eat.

To be honest, my appetite was null and void, but I knew that I needed to eat something. After my food arrived and it was time for the check, the waitress said, "You have a wonderful rest of your day ma'am."

Surprised, I asked her, "I'm sorry, where is the check? You never brought me the check." "It's already been taken care of. The lady sitting right across from the bar told me to tell you that she paid it forward. Have a great day!" Looking across at the bar, I didn't see anyone but men. I couldn't help but wonder whom it was that "paid it forward" for me. Whoever it was, I was grateful, and I knew that had to be a sign from God that things were going to be better for me.

Months had gone by and I had fallen into a deep and dark depression. I began to isolate myself from my family and friends, and I only spent time with my kids when I had to pick them up from school.

Finally deciding to begin picking up the pieces to my broken puzzle, I turned on the radio and a song from one of my favorite gospel artists began playing. As I heard the words, "Shattered, but I'm not broken," I heard the melody of her beautiful voice pierce my soul. As she continued to sing, I fell to my knees and surrendered all of my fears, all of my loneliness, all of my brokenness, all of my hurt, all of my pain, all of the blows to the face from Bryce's fist, all of the kicks to my stomach from Bryce's feet, all of the shoves and pushes from Bryce's hands, I finally gave it to God.

The more I cried, the louder she seemed to sing, and the louder she sang, the more I began to praise God and asked Him to deliver my soul and renew my spirit. Slowly I began to release all of my pain that I had suffered throughout the years and I heard God's voice say, "Let My will be done." In that moment, I allowed God's will to be done and, on that day, almost six months later, I took my life back.

I began spending more time with my children, I began completing tasks that I had once put on hold, I began to go out with my friends, and if they couldn't go I began treating myself. I began to live my life for Christine. I put myself through counseling and really began the transformation that I needed within my life.

I began working out to get my body back into shape and began getting my regular massage, hair, and nail appointments every month. I even started reading and writing more. I began reading the Bible not because I had never read it before, but I began reading for clarity and guidance on where I was in my life. I began applying those principles and lessons to my life so that I could really gain insight on who I was and where I was.

After three years of true healing from the inside out, I started focusing my attention on my business that I so desperately wanted to start years ago, but I never did. I wanted to use my struggle as story and my trials as a testimony for other women who were traveling down the road that I had so long ago traveled.

Volunteering down at the women's shelter one day, I ran into a familiar face. It caught me off guard, but when he walked up to me, I was so surprised that he remembered who I was after all of those years. "Miss Christine, how are you doing?" "Judge Snyder, I cannot believe that you remember me from all of these years. I know you see plenty of people with all of the cases you preside over. I'm great, I cannot complain. How have you been? What are you doing here?"

"Haha," he laughed. "I know it seems strange seeing a judge here at a women's shelter, but outside of sitting in court all day, I do have a bit of a life outside of this. I adopted this women's shelter over eight years ago so every other weekend I have dedicated a few hours here to help. What are you doing here?"

Smiling uncontrollably, I said, "Well, I started my own non-profit organization and I'm here to do volunteer work." With his nice pearly white teeth piercing through his smile, he said, "Oh wow, that is wonderful. These women could really use your services as well as your story." Staring at each other in a weird, flirtatious way, I said, "Well I should get going my time is up and I have another appointment that I must get to." In a hesitant way,

Judge Snyder said, "Oh, yes, of course. I will have to buy you coffee one day. Here is my card; call me some time."

Taking his card, I walked off and before I made it to the door he said, "Christine, there are certain people when you meet, you don't just forget, no matter how long it's been." Smiling, I walked out the door. When I made it to the car, I screamed. I didn't know what else to do.

You have to remember I didn't know how to flirt. I had been with Bryce since I was 18, so this was new to me, the whole "flirting" thing. But, if I had to guess if he was flirting, I do believe that's what he was doing. Gosh, I felt so lame, because I don't even know if I flirted back right with him.

The next day, I kept replaying our conversation over and over again, and I kept contemplating if I should call him or not. What would I say to him if he picked up? What if he didn't pick up? Is it just coffee or is it more? Nervous, scared, but still feeling bold, I called him. He picked up on the first ring as if he was expecting my call. With a strong, deep voice, he said, "I'm glad you called." Excited, yet anxious, I replied, "I am too."

Reflect on the following dating chronicle.

1. Have you ever had a moment where you decided to give up on love?

_____

_____

_____

_____

_____

_____

_____

_____

_____

_____

2. What steps have you taken to heal your mind, body, and spirit from a toxic relationship?

_____

_____

_____

_____

_____

_____

_____

_____

_____

3. Do you still believe in love? What are you doing to prepare yourself
   for it?

   _____

   _____

   _____

   _____

   _____

   _____

4. Abuse comes in many forms such as verbal, physical, and
   emotional. If you have ever experienced any form of abuse, then
   you understand the affects of it. As a beautiful queen, I want to
   encourage you to write yourself a note of encouragement and
   empowerment. You are worth it!

   _____

   _____

   _____

   _____

   _____

   _____

   _____

   _____

   _____

   _____

   _____

   _____

   _____

Chronicle
Five

The One

I was so proud of myself because I did not call him that night, I didn't even call the next day. I finally understood how to stop placing others before me. I was so tired of repeating the same cycles with these guys and I knew that if I wanted a different response, I had to be different.

I called him two days later and I started the conversation with, "I was just calling to let you know that I made it home safely." I think that caught him off guard because I just knew that he was expecting me to call him that same night when we left the party.

He walked in all dressed up eyeing me, telling jokes and laughing all loud. I just ignored him because I had already heard about how he was the 'ladies' man and I just didn't have time for the games.

That night, he pressed so hard to get my number to the point where he just finally wrote his number down on a card and put it inside of my car. He was a little annoyed that I didn't give him my number up front, but honestly, I think that small action is what hooked him and kept him interested in wanting to get to know me even more.

That day we talked on the phone for hours and I must admit, I was feeling comfortable; however, I was not willing to let my guard down so easily with him. He said, "Look, I really enjoyed talking your ear off today, but I really do want to see you again. How about an official date?" Excited, yet calm, I replied, "And where exactly would you like to take me for a first date?" "Well, you know the fair is in town for the next few weeks, so why don't we do that on tomorrow?"

"That sounds cool, I'm down for that." "Cool, so I can pick you up on tomorrow and then we can do the park and ride since it will more than likely be super crowded. Is that cool with you?" "Of course, that should be fine. Just remember to text when you are on your way so that you are not waiting until tomorrow for me to come out the house," I said laughing through the phone. Our date to the fair was cool; we ate really good, had some great conversation, and had a real fun time with one another.

After our first date to the fair, I invited him over so that he could meet my mother. It was the first time in a long time that I had allowed a guy to come over and meet my mother. When she walked in to the living room, he stood up and said, "Hello, Ms. Smith, it's so nice to finally meet you!" Now if you know anything about my mother, she is 4 feet and 9 inches tall but she has a very strong personality. She is a no-nonsense woman and says what she means and means what she says. She stepped back and looked him up and down and said, "I know you."

At that point, I was so embarrassed and confused; he started looking around because he was trying to figure out how she knew him, so I finally said, "What do you mean, Mama?" She stated again, "I know you, what is your name and what do you do for a living?" When he told her his name and what he did for a living, she said, "Uh-huh" and walked off.

We both just stood there in disbelief. It was so bad I had to apologize to him because it just got so awkward. Once he left, she came out the room and I asked her why she was so rude. She said, "Please tell him I am so sorry, I was not trying to be rude, but I dreamed about him a couple of days ago and I was taken aback because that was him!" I looked at her, and she proceeded to say, "He was dressed up in a suit and he had a briefcase, so when he told me he was a real estate broker, I just had to walk off because he was the man that I saw with you in my dreams."

We sat there in shock, and I couldn't believe that the man she had dreamed about for me was the man she had met in her living room. Talk about surreal!

Time went on and we hit it off with each other pretty well. For the first time in a long time, I could honestly say that I was happy just being able to date someone with no strings attached. I did not have to worry about paying for every date, I did not have to pick him up and drop him off, I did not have to worry about baby mama drama; everything was just so different. We had so much in common, and many of our goals and aspirations were aligned. It felt as if we had known each other our entire lives.

One night after we left his church banquet, we went back to his mom's house and oddly enough, we figured out why we felt like we had known each other our whole life.

We began talking about my cousin, and ironically, his mother said that she knew her, and they were really good friends. She said, "Oh yes, we always hang out at least once a month because we are always doing some type of get together."

I laughed and said, "Well, I am almost certain that we have all been out together because I am typically always hanging out with my cousin. Anytime she goes out or is having something, she always calls and asks if I want to join."

While we continued the conversation, his mother made her way to her coffee table and began flipping through some old photos. As she continued to flip through the pictures, I saw me! I said, "Hold on, that's me right there!" I was so shocked and couldn't believe it! We all began to laugh because there I was standing right next to his mother in the photo posing and smiling cheek-to-cheek. His mom said, "Now, this is crazy. Do ya'll know this picture has been sitting on this coffee table for at least six years?"

At that moment, I couldn't help but think to myself, "Could he be the one for me?" I instantly found myself getting ready to repeat the same cycle of moving too fast. I told myself, "No more fairytale, this is reality!" Just like that I had to snap myself into reality and continue to understand, listen, and be patient.

As time went on, we began to see each other more often, and we found ourselves spending a lot of time together. Slowly but surely, I began to notice little things that I didn't like. He would always turn his phone upside down; he would always hold on to his phone as if he didn't want to let it out of his sight; he would also take calls away from where I was, and I found all of these behaviors to be strange.

I started to become suspicious of other women being in the picture. I'm not going to lie to you, I was naïve and told myself that this was just his thing, even though I knew these actions were all red flags and signs of another woman being in the picture. In that moment, I found myself excusing his behaviors because I did not want to feel lonely again. I wanted to force this new relationship to work.

I began reflecting on all the hard work I had put into myself and how far I had come. I then reflected on how God equipped me with the will and strength to move away from that dark cloud from my life. I literally told myself, "Girl, you are not about to put yourself through any more of ignoring the signs!" I could no longer be afraid of what the truth could be or fear being lonely. I knew that I had to put my worth first by not allowing my intuition to be overpowered by great conversation and quality time.

I knew if I wanted this relationship to work, I had to do the opposite of what I would normally have done in past situations. The first time I questioned him about all the different women popping up on his phone, he simply justified them all as his friends or clients. "These are girls that I went to school with and just catching up with them. You know I'm in real estate, right? So, a lot of these friends are clients that I work with." Although the story seemed solid, and I did look over it, I still kept all of his patterns and red flags in the back of my head.

Several months passed by, and we were still going strong--so strong that he still hadn't made me his girlfriend. I found this to be strange because I couldn't understand how you could date someone for eight months and not want to be in a relationship. It wasn't until I was talking to my coworker, and he made me put some things into perspective.

He said, "Look, I'm going to tell you straight like this. If ya'll been 'dating' for eight months and he still hasn't made you his girlfriend, it's almost certain it's because he has other women around him that he is still entertaining. Most men do not take that long to figure out what they want because from the moment we see ya'll, we pretty much know exactly what we want from ya'll, so just keep your eyes open."

Although I had already known these things and this was nothing new to me, these words for some reason seemed so iconic. I really began to do some serious praying, meditating, and writing to journal my thoughts out. I knew things were not right within our dating relationship, and I really had to ask myself, was I going to continue to allow a man to not know and understand my worth. Better yet, was I going to continue to allow myself to not know my own worth?

I could honestly say the reason why I did not confront the issues with him was because I felt in my spirit that my feelings about him would be right, and I just could not bear to feel that pain again. Then I asked myself, "Would you rather know now and change the situation, or would you rather be in denial and let this man parade whoever he wants in and around him and you?" I put my strong face on and confronted this situation head on.

A few days after I was forced to sit in my own thoughts, God allowed me to hear and see exactly what I needed.

It was early Saturday morning, and his phone rang, "Hello," I heard him say. "Give me a few minutes; let me go down here and check." He said, "Hey baby, this is my homeboy and he said it's urgent. I'll be downstairs on this call, do you want me to make you some tea?" I instantly became suspicious because I knew him well enough to know that he NEVER explained himself. See, he was the type of guy that didn't need approval from anyone. He did what he wanted when he wanted and wasn't apologetic for it. So with observing him and knowing his patterns, my B.S. meter was sky high. I replied to him, "No. I'm just going to lie down and stay in the bed, I'm not feeling too well." As soon as he made his way downstairs and I didn't hear his voice anymore, I made my way downstairs.

There he was in the office with the door cracked and on the phone, and let's just say it wasn't his homeboy. After a few minutes of hearing him on this call with this other woman, I just opened the door and said, "I sure hope she was worth all of this. You enjoy the rest of your day." I walked out that house and never looked back.

That was one of the hardest things I had to do, because I really did care so much about him. I knew that if I wanted him to be my husband, I had to let him go. For once, I made the decision for me. I didn't consider what he would think when I walked away. I didn't give him an opportunity to explain because if I had, I would have been right back there in his arms allowing him to explain and excusing his behavior.

Most importantly, I didn't allow pity for myself; instead, I made him chase me. He now had to show me that he loved and cared about me a little bit more than I loved and cared about him.

Three months went by with no communication between us. He would send back-to- back messages and voicemails at the beginning, and then it slowly stopped. I think he got the picture that I wasn't trying to hear anything from him.

During this time, I cried, and I wrote, and I cried some more, and then I cried again until there were no more tears left.

Slowly, I started to regain focus on all the things that were important and what I wanted. Then out of the blue, my phone rang and it was him.

After three whole months, I finally decided to answer the phone. With no hello or awkward silence, he asked, "What all do you want to know?" I was thrown off guard by the question and I said, "Excuse me?" He said, "What do you want to know?" I know that I have hurt you and there is no excuse for it, so I want you to ask me anything you want to know about me because I can't bear losing you again." He continued, "In this moment, right now, and from here on out, I will do whatever it takes to be with you." I sat there very quiet for a few seconds and I finally just asked, " Why?" Although I was hesitant, I asked because I wanted to know that the man I loved was really someone who was worth loving.

During that conversation, he revealed a lot. I didn't know whether or not to scream, cry, leave, stay, get pissed, curse him out, or be thankful! I mean how much dirt could someone actually do. Once he finished revealing his true self to me, I could hear and feel the burden being lifted off of his shoulders. For the first time in a long time, he became so transparent that I could see through him. In that moment, we actually healed together.

As time went on, he began to make those necessary changes not only for him and me, but also for our relationship, and I knew he was the one because at the end of it all, he changed for me. He told me that he knew from the moment he first saw me at the party that he was going to marry me and that if I would allow him to show me that he was worth my loving him again, he would do whatever necessary to protect me, my heart, and our relationship.

We began to work on rebuilding our trust. That was the hardest part for me because everybody knows once trust has been broken, it is hard to gain it back.

To make me feel secure, he started leaving his phone open, to the point where I had complete access to it. He began communicating more with me about his whereabouts. Instead of saying, "I'll be out late" or "I'm running errands," he would tell me the time and place of where and with whom he would be. He started bringing me around his close friends, and I was now being introduced as his girlfriend-- not just Ayanna.

We started working out of different couples' self-help books so that we could begin exploring one another on a different, more intimate level. We also began to complete goal-setting activities with one another. We would take quiet time together and write out our short-term and long-term goals. Then we would post them and begin completing tasks that we had set forth.

We started having discussions about marriage, children, and our futures together. Most importantly, he began to profess his love for me both publically and privately. He promised me that he would never do anything to lose me again.

In this moment I realized that in order for us to be complete for each other, we both had to heal.

During this time we discovered and uncovered many challenges from our past that we had to heal from. We fulfilled this by going through our marriage counseling sessions and in time, we both began to see new growth within our relationship. Within the months to come, on New Year's Eve of 2015, Tim proposed to me in front of our family and friends. On August 7, 2016, we became Mr. and Mrs. Jackson!

Reflect on the following dating chronicle.

1. What steps have you taken to position yourself for 'The One'?

_____

_____

_____

_____

_____

_____

_____

_____

_____

_____

2. Have you ever been afraid of walking away from 'The One'? What helped you get through it? Why didn't you walk away?

_____

_____

_____

_____

_____

_____

_____

_____

_____

_____

3. How important is it for you to know your self-worth?

_____
_____
_____
_____
_____
_____
_____
_____
_____
_____

4. What behaviors have you excused? What's the worst that could happen if all of your questions were answered honestly?

_____
_____
_____
_____
_____
_____
_____
_____
_____
_____
_____
_____
_____

The Breakthrough

My hope, for every woman that has read this book, is to have an epic breakthrough. I hope in this time, you have recognized yourself in one of the characters mentioned above. Within this reflection, I hope that you were able to take away the bad and turn it into something good. I hope that you were able to gain insight on women who are just like you.

I want you to know that in your moment of singleness, loneliness, abandonment, frustration, unworthiness, and all the other negative emotions that you may be currently feeling, or have felt, that you find great value and power within these chronicles.

No, every woman did not have a success story with a fairytale ending. Unfortunately, that is not how life works and it is just not how the cards are always dealt. Some of these women had to go through the storm to see the rainbow on the other side.

However, if you apply the many lessons taught to you through each of these chronicles, you will see a light at the end of your tunnel. Though some of these chronicles were challenging to write, I knew they would be beneficial to many women who are just like me.

Your breakthrough is coming ladies! Mr. Right is on his way to find you. In the meantime, continue to prepare your mind, body, and spirit by Finding Boldness Excellence And Uniqueness Through You!

In the space below, I challenge you to write a special note to 'The One.' Be sure to date and time-stamp it.

He is closer than you could ever imagine!

_____

_____

_____

_____

_____

_____

_____

_____

_____

_____

_____

_____

_____

_____

_____

_____

_____

_____

_____

_____

_____